W9-CEK-006

Margarita's Star

Written by David Ira Rottenberg

Illustrated by Eliza Rose David

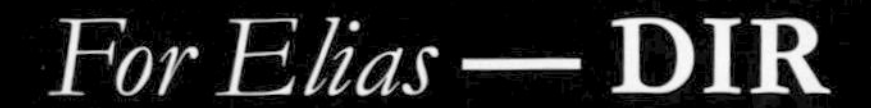

For Elias — **DIR**

For Mom, Dad, and Alex — **ERD**

Cedar Crest Books
Natick, MA USA
www.cedarcrestbooks.com

Maragarita's Star
Story by: David Ira Rottenberg
Illustrations by: Eliza Rose David

Margarita's Star was inspired by the beautiful poem, "A Margarita Debayle," by Nicaraguan poet Rubén Dario (1867-1916).

Cover Design: Eliza Rose David
Book Design: Eliza Rose David

First Printing – April 2017

ISBN: 978-0-910291-18-7

Production Date: April 2017
Plant & Location: Printed by Everbest Printing (Guangzhou, China), Co. Ltd
Batch Number: 78942-0

Margarita's Star

Margarita is a princess,

quick, graceful, and mischievous.

She lives in a wondrous palace made of
coral, marble, and pearl.

One night, she gazes out her bedroom window.
"The stars are so pretty," she thinks...
"prettier than the jewels my father gives me.
What if I take a few? Who will ever miss any?"

The next moment, Margarita searches in her closet...

for her lightest shoes – the silk ones with pink ribbons that make her feet feel like wings.

Slipping them on, she climbs the tallest tower in the palace...

and dances until she
soars away on
the wind.

She flies over forests, mountains, and seas...

past the moon and up to the top of the sky.

The stars glitter before her like silver flowers...

and she plucks all she can hold in her hands and pockets.

In the glow of the moonlight,
she returns to the palace...

heaping the stars onto the table where she dresses.

Sewing the stars together with golden thread, Margarita adorns her hair, ears, and neck.

Staring into the mirror,
the princess admires
herself. The stars
dazzle and blaze
all around her face.

The night of the carnival,
noblemen and women...

swing arm-in-arm across
the ballroom floor.

But everyone stops and gasps
when Margarita enters.

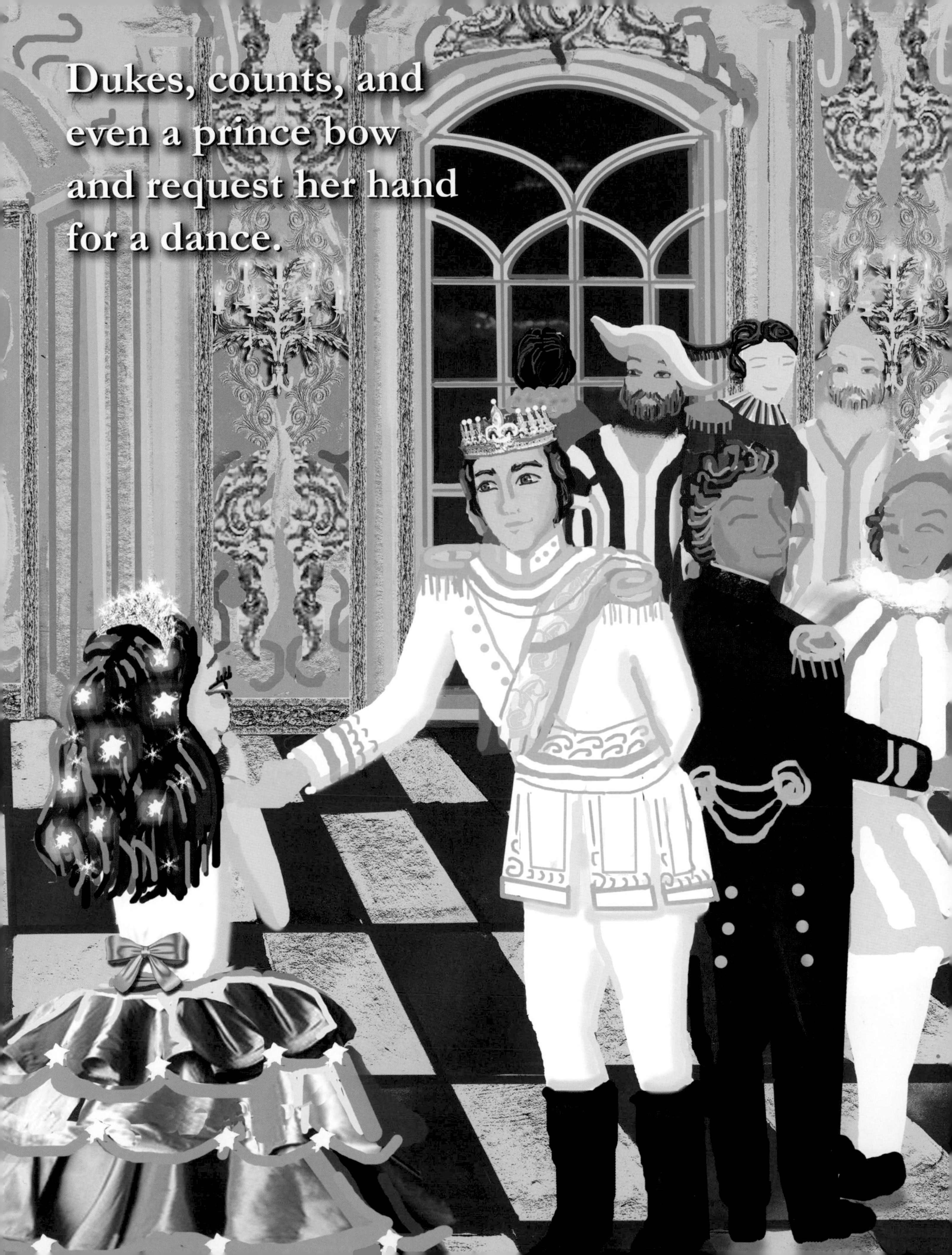

Dukes, counts, and even a prince bow and request her hand for a dance.

At midnight, forty trumpets announce the king. Trembling with excitement...

Margarita approaches her father. But when she kneels before him, he frowns.

"How did you get this jewelry of stars?" he demands. Margarita tells the truth. "The stars are so pretty — I flew on the wind and plucked them from the sky." The king sighs. He is firm when it comes to right and wrong....

"Do you not know –
stars guide sailors across the sea...

And
Inspire
Poets to
Write
Sweet
Verses

Stars coax lovers to give their hearts...

and twinkle for children to wish their **BIGGEST** wishes.

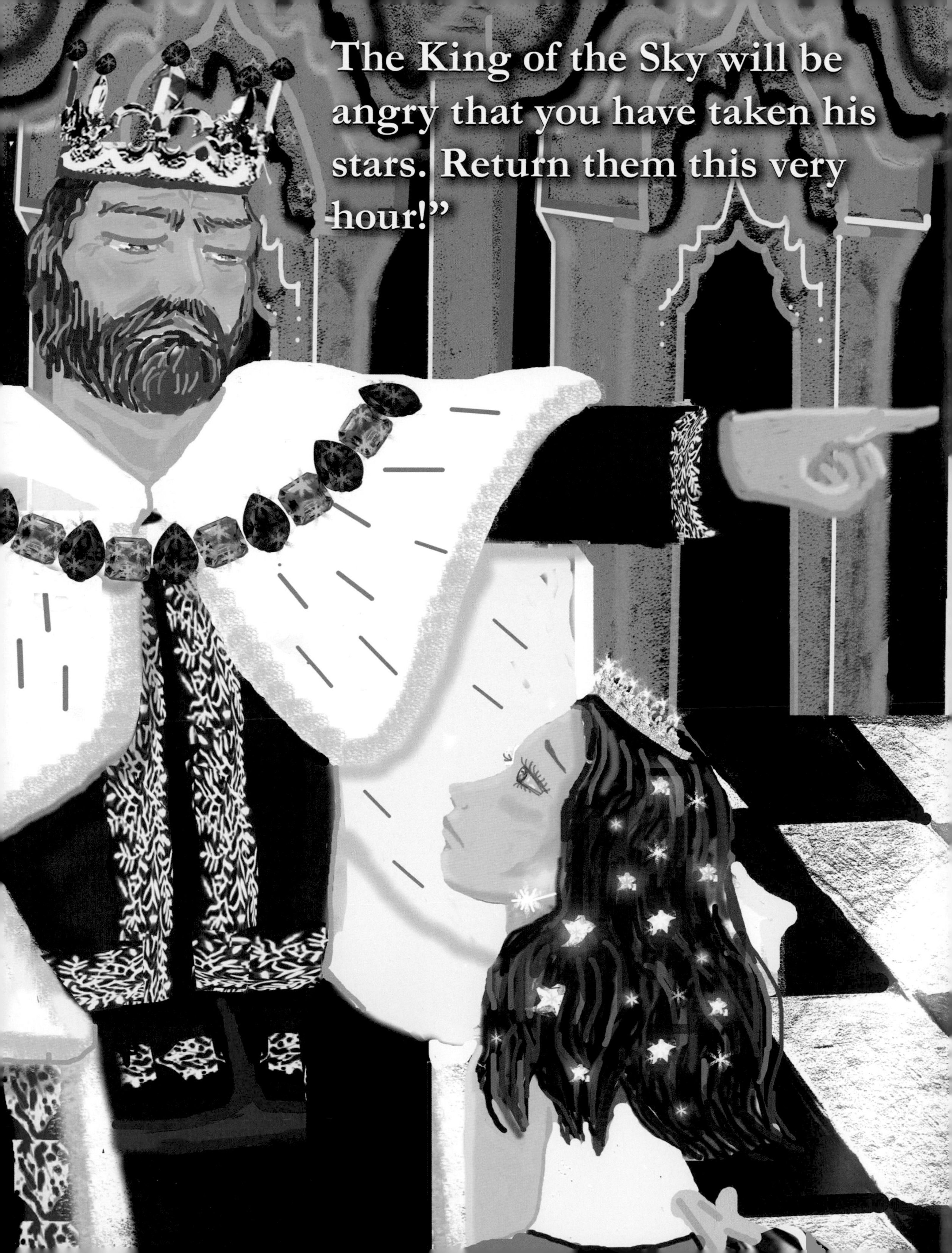

The King of the Sky will be angry that you have taken his stars. Return them this very hour!”

Margarita is sad, but
she climbs the tower
and leaps on the
wind...
wheeling like a bird into the
darkness and far beyond.

Breaking the golden threads,
she fastens the stars back
above the moon.

But the stars wobble and slip,
falling like petals down
to her feet.

Margarita does not want to
disappoint her father and
sticks the stars up again and
again until she cannot raise
her arms.

Then, as if in a dream, the King of the Sky appears and whispers as softly as a feather.

"Do not worry, Margarita. The stars are my flowers. They shine from joy. I know where each belongs."

He reaches out his hands, which are made of light and fixes every star in its rightful place.

"Here is one star," he says. "It is lovely, bright, and true, like you. Keep it near to remember this night."

Clutching her star,
Margarita glides back to
her wondrous palace.

In his velvet robes of crimson,
purple, and green,
Margarita's
father marches
up the tower.

As soon as Margarita's toes touch the ground, he hugs her and smiles his proudest smile.

He does not mind that she keeps one star – the King of the Sky gave it to her.

Years pass and Margarita marries her prince.

But the King of Sky still visits her dreams... and she still remembers his words.

Every morning when she awakes, Margarita lifts the star from its box and pins it as a promise over her heart.